FUN WITH
❧ Franklin ❧
Trace and Colour Book

Based on the books
Written by Paulette Bourgeois
Illustrated by Brenda Clark

Kids Can Press Ltd. acknowledges with appreciation the assistance of the Canada Council and the Ontario Arts Council in the production of this book.

ISBN   1-55074-396-1

Text copyright © 1997 by Paulette Bourgeois
Illustrations copyright © 1997 by Brenda Clark
Interior illustrations executed by Shelley Southern, based on original drawings by Brenda Clark.

Franklin and the Franklin character are trade marks of Kids Can Press Ltd.

Kids Can Press Ltd.
29 Birch Avenue
Toronto, Ontario, Canada
M4V 1E2

Printed and bound in Canada by Kromar Printing Limited

97 0 9 8 7 6 5 4 3 2 1

Illustrations by Shelley Southern

Kids Can Press Ltd., Toronto

Follow the instructions below to make your own Franklin picture. To begin, gently tear out a piece of tracing paper from the centre of this book.

Choose a face on page 4 or 5. Place the tracing paper over it, and check that you have enough room to include Franklin's body too. Trace Franklin's face. Try not to move the paper as you trace.

Now choose a body from page 6, 7 or 8. Before you begin tracing, make sure Franklin's body will connect with his head.

Next trace some of Franklin's friends or family from pages 9, 10, 11 and 12.

d something from Franklin's forest on ge 13.

Finish your picture by tracing one of Franklin's favourite things from page 14.

ow make a picture of Franklin playing.

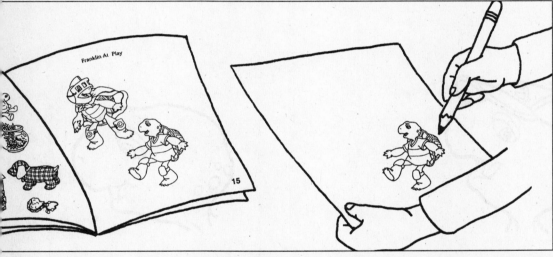

On a clean piece of tracing paper, trace a picture of Franklin from page 15.

Complete your picture by adding some of Franklin's playthings from page 16.

You can make lots of other pictures by tracing different drawings. Mix and match drawings any funny way you like. And don't forget to colour your pictures!

Franklin Faces

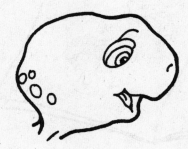

Franklin Funny Faces

Franklin Bodies

Franklin Funny Bodies

More Funny Bodies

Franklin's Best Friend

Franklin's Friends and Family

More Friends and Family

Franklin's Forest

Franklin's Favourite Things

Franklin at Play

Franklin's Playthings